THE TALE OF
Wagmore Gently

LINDA ASHMAN

ILLUSTRATED BY
JOHN BENDALL-BRUNELLO

Dutton Children's Books ◉ **New York**

Text copyright © 2002 by Linda Ashman
Illustrations copyright © 2002 by John Bendall-Brunello
All rights reserved.

CIP Data is available.

Published in the United States 2002 by Dutton Children's Books,
a division of Penguin Putnam Books for Young Readers
345 Hudson Street, New York, New York 10014
www.penguinputnam.com
Designed by Richard Amari
Printed in Hong Kong
First Edition
10 9 8 7 6 5 4 3 2 1
ISBN 0-525-46916-8

To my siblings,
Vince, Leslie, and Liz,
and in remembrance of our beloved Pepper

And to Nicky, because she **IS** Wagmore,
and to Remy, just because

L.A.

For Sammy and, as ever, Tiziana

J.B.

Meet Wagmore,
a happy dog with a powerful tail…

...which sometimes makes his family very unhappy.
One wag can wake the deepest sleeper.

A mere twitch can wreck a game of checkers.

And a few blissful thumps can spoil a fine musical performance.

One morning, Wagmore's wildly wagging tail lopped off the zinnias, scattered Bertha's kitty litter, and woke up the baby.

Mr. Gently was furious. He threatened to keep Wagmore home from the Trail Trekkers outing the next day if he didn't control his tail.

Miss his favorite hike? That made Wagmore sad.
He slipped away to the den, his tail drooping like a
wilted daisy.

But the sight of his favorite chair made him wag so hard he sent the table lamp crashing to the floor. Bertha the cat, disgusted by his lack of control, directed him to some self-help books.

Wagology Made Easy

Wagging~Vol 2

7 steps to a SAFER TAIL

Taming the WOLF Within

Wagmore spent the day reading, pausing every so often to practice his tail-taming exercises.

When his tail twitched at the idea of a romp with Jack, he pictured a pack of scary dogs instead.

When it wriggled at the prospect of a delicious meal, he forced himself to think of something far less appetizing.

When it thumped at the thought of a warm, soft bed, he imagined the cold, hard floor of a doghouse.

The next morning, while the Trail Trekkers checked their supplies, Mr. Gently gave Wagmore a stern reminder to control his tail.

Wagmore vowed to remain wag-free. He was certain
he'd conquered his problem at last.

The Trail Trekkers began marching up the hill. Jack, a budding ornithologist, lagged behind, scanning the trees for exotic birds. Suddenly he spotted a red tail feather through the leaves. He crept through the brush for a closer look.

Wagmore loved blazing new trails. But he remembered his vow to restrain his tail and quashed his joy with a negative thought.

The bird hopped along the edge of a cliff and then disappeared. Jack crawled along the ledge, grabbing a branch to steady himself. All at once, the branch gave way and Jack tumbled down the hill.

That looks like fun!

YYYIIIKES!

Wagmore was thrilled at the thought of rolling in the grass but fought the urge to wag. He fought it so hard, in fact, he didn't realize that Jack was in trouble.

The grass is infested with bloodthirsty fleas.

The grass is infested with bloodthirsty fleas.

The grass is infested with bloodthirsty fleas.

Jack rolled straight into the river. Wagmore found swimming in fast-flowing rapids particularly exhilarating but remembered Mr. Gently's warning and concentrated on thinking terrible thoughts. He concentrated so hard he didn't even notice the fear on Jack's face.

Faster, Wagmore!

When Wagmore finally realized that Jack needed help, he paddled him back to shore. They sat by the river, resting.

"Thanks, Wagmore," said Jack. "You saved me."

Wagmore liked feeling appreciated. He liked it so much he couldn't think of a single unpleasant thought. His tail quivered.

"We're lost, Wagmore," said Jack. "You've got to get
us out of this canyon."

Wagmore loved feeling needed. He struggled to
stifle his happiness, but his willpower was weakening.
His tail twitched harder.

"I'm scared," said Jack. He gave Wagmore a hug. Wagmore loved hugs more than Bow-Wow Beefy Bones. His tail trembled wildly.

He curled up in a ball and focused all his energy on being miserable.

Then Jack rubbed his belly.

It was too much. Wagmore's tail hit the stream so
hard it sent a blast of water shooting high into the air.

Chopper One to Ranger Station.
No sign of missing boy and canine,
but I've spotted some sort of geyser.

A rescue helicopter flying overhead swooped down
to take a closer look.

Jack heard the helicopter above the roar of Wagmore's splashing tail. He waved his arms and shouted.

The pilot landed and airlifted Jack and Wagmore to
the top of the hill, where the Trail Trekkers huddled,
waiting for news of their lost companions.

The Trekkers were overjoyed to see Jack and Wagmore leap from the helicopter.

The warm welcome made Wagmore forget all about restraining his tail. He wagged so hard he snapped a sapling in half and sent leaves flying everywhere. For once, Mr. Gently didn't mind.

News of the rescuc spread quickly. Reporters and camera crews flocked to the house to meet the heroic dog. Wagmore, delighted, no longer bothered to contain his joy.

The Forest Rescue Squad had a party in Wagmore's honor. The whole town came, which of course made Wagmore very happy.

Best of all, Wagmore's family stopped scolding him for his unruly tail. In fact, they found it could be quite useful. On hot summer days, for example.

And cleaning day.

And once they bought some earmuffs...

and rearranged the furniture,

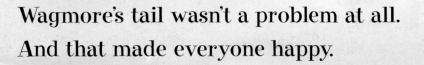

Wagmore's tail wasn't a problem at all.
And that made everyone happy.

Especially Wagmore.